What You Can Do, I Can Too

By Helen Vallaeys
Illustrated by Dani Ward

Printed in the United States of America
First Printing, 2019
ISBN 978-0-578-46170-0
www.helenvallaeys.com

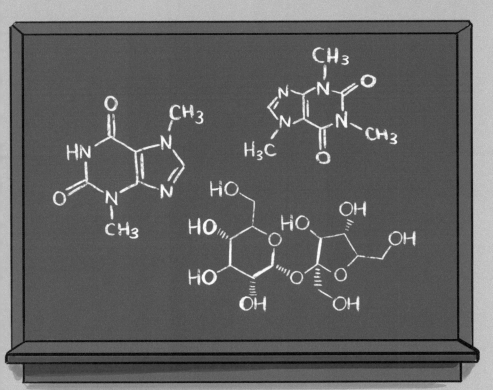

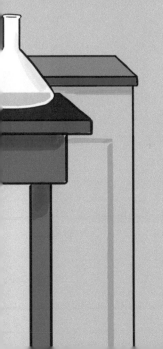

It's bright and early, and scientist Jo
is dressed in her coat, ready to go.
She works in a lab doing what she knows best,
measuring, mixing, and running some tests.
Her goal is to someday discover a cure
for an illness no one should have to endure.
She carefully places small drops on plates,
when she hears the alarm and evacuates.

The fire truck rushes with its siren blaring,
and as it arrives the flames are flaring.
Firefighter Aiko, in her fireproof clothes,
quickly jumps down and grabs the hose.
Water shoots out and battles the flames,
and Aiko keeps calm while she carefully aims.
The ambulance arrives to promptly zoom,
anyone injured to the Emergency Room.

Doctor Roz and her team are on high alert,
ready to help all those who are hurt.
She examines her patient, runs some tests,
asks a few questions, and listens to her chest.
She looks in her ears, shines a light in each eye,
and makes sure her blood pressure isn't too high.
She's focused on her work and completely ignores,
the noise coming from the builders next door.

On the construction site Lexi talks to her crew,
reviews the plans and explains what to do.
To be seen and protected, she is safely dressed,
in her hard hat, boots, and bright yellow vest.
Soon this building must stand tall and strong,
so Lexi is busy with moving things along.
She directs the crane and looks up to the sky,
just in time to see a plane flying by.

Up high in the sky pilot Liz steers the plane,
and grips the controls as they near thunder and rain.
She says on the speaker: "It's a bumpy flight,
so fasten your seat belt low and tight!"
She flies over mountains, cities, and towns,
and a few hours later, her plane touches down.
Passenger Jenna wishes Liz a nice day,
but she is late for work, so rushes away.

Jenna is a judge who helps decide,
between two people who is wrong, who is right.
Her role is to listen to everyone there
and make decisions that are just and fair.
With a gavel in her hand, dressed in a gown,
she sits high on a bench and looks around.
Meanwhile, officer Jill stands at attention,
in case there's a problem that needs intervention.

Back at the station the other officers meet,
and hear that athletes are in town to compete.
Chief Jada announces: "Let's keep everyone safe
and give people a warning if they don't behave."
She shows on the board who needs to help where,
while police dog Roxy, sits alert and prepared.
"And," says Jada, "bring your handcuffs and vests,
because we may have to make some arrests."

Athletes in the arena are ready to go,
with hurdle jumping, pole vault, and javelin throw.
Becca grabs her pole and is about to begin,
she has trained for months and hopes to win.
The audience cheers as runners go by,
and watches as Becca gives the pole vault a try.
On the sidelines reporters are there to record,
the winners of the day and how much they scored.

In the studio, Mia reports the news
with help from Bill and the camera crew.
"We are going live", they hear someone say,
and Mia shares the events of the day.
She talks about the world, weather, and sports
when they hear about an update the White House reports.
She says: "Bill, let's go over there,
to see what the president has to share."

It's bustling in the White House briefing room
when agent Ava hears the event will start soon.
She looks around to make sure there's no threat
to visitors, staff, or the president.
She's focused and alert, with a watchful eye,
on all that goes on and whoever walks by.
When someone announces: "We're ready to begin,"
the room goes quiet and the president comes in.

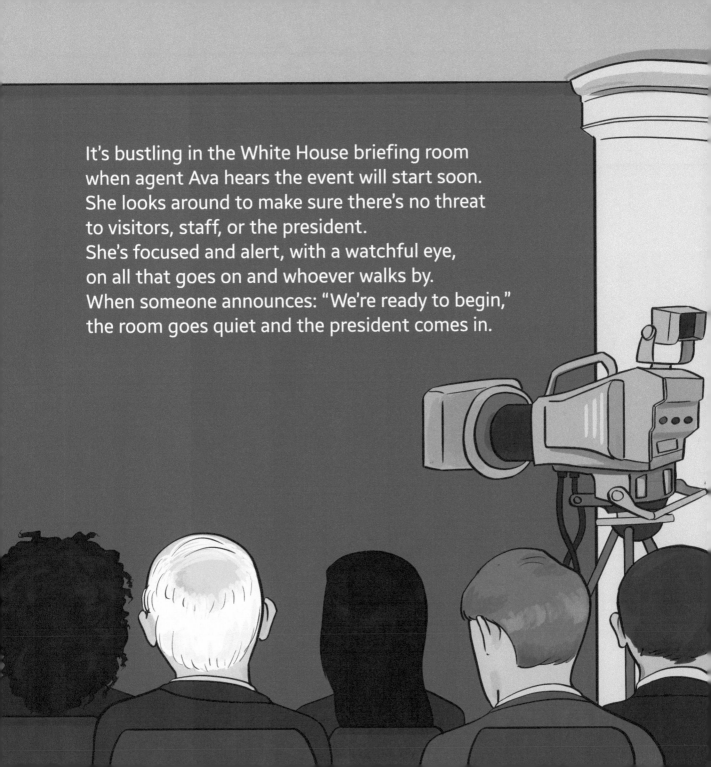

Home from school in the afternoon,
Naya and Finn sit in the living room.
They flip through the channels when Naya asks Finn,
"What would you be if you could be anything?"
He says: "An astronaut! I'd fly to Mars,
pass by the moon and touch the stars."
Naya nods, then looks at Finn to say:
"I'm gonna be the president one day!"

What are YOU going to be one day?

CPSIA information can be obtained
at www.ICGtesting.com
Printed in the USA
LVHW071213120519
617531LV00027B/1331/P